Dedication

For Piper & Londyn
xoxo
Mimi

I also want to thank my Mom
for her encouragement, love, and support.
xoxo
Teresa

The author gratefully acknowledges the artistic contribution of Aneeza Ashraf

Copyright © 2020 by Teresa Hunt
All rights reserved. This book or any portion thereof may not be reproduced or used in any manner whatsoever without the express written permission of the publisher except for the use of brief quotations in a book review.

Don't miss these other Piperlicious books!

Piperlicious Ocean Adventure!

Piperlicious & Her Critter Friends!

For more Piperlicious fun, visit Piperlicious.com

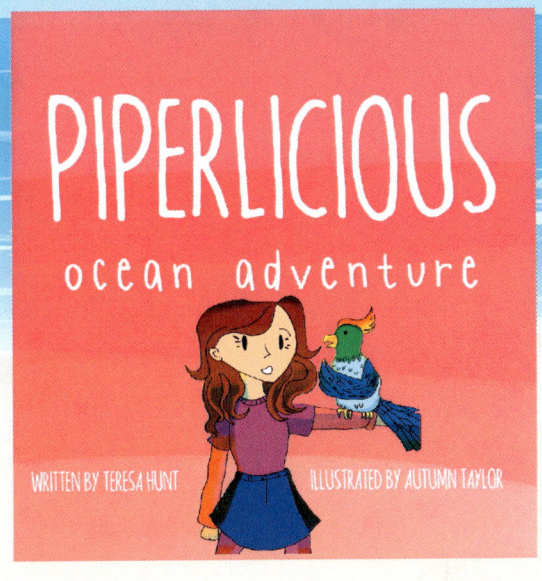
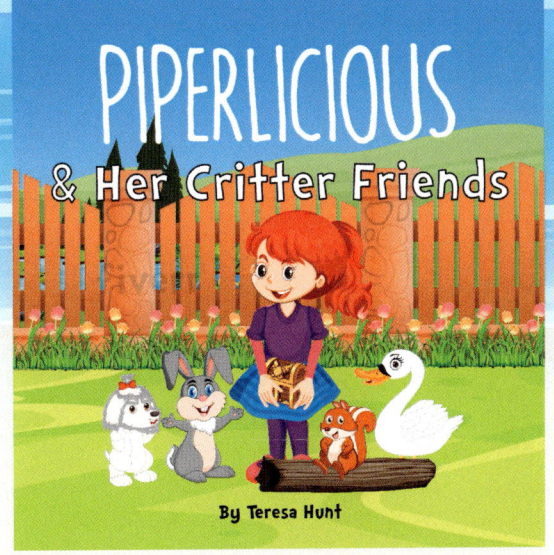

"Piperlicious! You won't believe it!" Mimi's voice called.

Piperlicious back from a daydream. It was a good daydream! Piperlicious, her little sister, Londyn, and their pet monkey, Paz, had been looking for pirate treasure on a magical island. Piperlicious had been reading about a 170-year-old pirate treasure that was just off the coast of Hawaii.

Piperlicious wanted to go treasure-hunting so badly!

"Coming, Grandma!" she called back, running down and giving Mimi a big hug.

"You've won!" said Mimi proudly, waving a postcard. "That story you wrote for the National Feed American Children competition won first prize!"

"Yay!" said Piperlicious happily.

"Well done, Piperlicious," said Londyn. "What's her prize, Mimi?"

"Let's see," said Mimi, reading the card. "You've won... oh, my goodness! You've won an all-expenses paid trip to the prize-giving which will be at Kauwela Palace!"

Mimi looked at her grand-daughters, seeing that they didn't understand.

"That's in Hawaii! The King and Queen are going to do the presentation!"

The next few weeks went by quickly, while Mimi booked the tickets and sent off all the paperwork, and Piperlicious even had her picture in the local newspaper! Piperlicious made up a little song that she sang all the time!

"I'm going to Hawaii,
I'll meet the King and Queen
A super fun vacation!
I'm going to Hawaii
A surf and fun vacation!
We're all going to Hawaii!"

"I'm going to Hawaii,
I'll meet the King and Queen
A super fun vacation!

NEWSPAPER

www.newspaper.com

Dallas, Texas, Sunday, January 1, 2020 , Volume 2, Number 1 • SPECIAL EDITION

Piperlicious WINNER of all-expenses paid trip to Kauwela Palace!

I'm going to Hawaii
A surf and fun vacation!
We're all going to Hawaii!"

In Piperlicious's bedroom there was great excitement amongst Piperlicious's and Londyn's secret friends. They sang the song with Piperlicious when she sang it, and fell silent when someone who wasn't Piperlicious or Londyn came in. (That's why they were secret friends, only Piperlicious and Londyn knew about them!) They had all heard the news and they were very excited! Especially as some of them would be going too! But even the friends that would be staying helped Piperlicious to pack!

While Red Suitcase stretched open luxuriously on the bed, Wardrobe and Chest of Drawers sent T-shirts and shorts dancing over the carpet onto the bed where they folded themselves neatly into the case, tucking in tightly to make room.

Piperlicious and Londyn were the only people that the secret friends would talk too. If anyone else came into the bedroom, they would go very quiet and still!

Finally, it was time to go! Piperlicious carefully packed Paz into the side pocket of her purse. "Ooh, squashed!" he said, squirming to get comfortable.

Then Piperlicious packed the last few items into Red Suitcase, making sure that Sony Camera was far away from Fuji Filmier (Fuji's job was filming everything Piperlicious did on vacation) – the last time those two had been allowed to travel together, they'd both wasted their batteries taking pictures and videos of each other! They wanted Piperlicious's attention all the time, so they had to be kept apart!

On the plane, Londyn and Piperlicious chatted to each about what they wanted to do when they were in Hawaii. Mimi sat in between Londyn and Piperlicious holding a grass skirt in her hands.

Londyn asked, "What's that, Mimi?"
Piperlicious said "It's a grass skirt! They wear them in Hawaii to do hula dances!"

"That's right, Piperlicious," said Mimi, making the skirt dance by moving her hands up and down. The sisters laughed to see it, then listened as Mimi told the story of how she had visited Hawaii for a little while as a girl, and had won a Hula competition. She loved hulas, she said, and luaus too! Mom and Dad were behind them, listening too.

Piperlicious said that Mimi was better entertainment than the in-flight movie that was playing, and Londyn nodded in agreement!

When they landed, there was someone waiting for them! It was a young girl who said "Aloha," then told them she was a kaikamahine, or girl, who worked as a traditional greeter. She placed a flowery lei around Piperlicious's neck and sang her a welcome song.

Piperlicious was a little bit embarrassed by all the attention, but she loved it too, her face turning almost as red as her hair with excitement! Londyn clapped her hands and jumped up and down with excitement too: she couldn't wait for the adventure they would have.

Before the greeter could walk them to the limo that would take them to the palace, Piperlicious saw two of her secret friends squirming about!

Red Suitcase had been squashed in the hold, and she was now so full of energy and excitement that she couldn't keep still, while Brown Bag was Piperlicious's carry-on bag and was exhausted! She had been walked on, kicked, sat on, and dropped. A lot!

Brown Bag wailed, "I just want to sit quietly for a moment, but Red Suitcase won't stop running around! I'm never going on vacation again!"

Piperlicious soothed her friends and asked them to stay calm just for a little while longer – they were nearly there. Red Suitcase nodded, and Brown Bag gave a big sigh, and then agreed to be good. Piperlicious stroked them gently as she guided them into the royal limo.

They went straight to the Palace to say hello to the King and Queen. While they waited in the large hall, Piperlicious spun on her toes, her arms stretched up to the high ceiling and wide walls.

"The Palace is amazing!" she gasped. "It's the most beautiful palace in the whole world, with its crystal and gold chandeliers, ornate jewel-toned walls, and red carpet! Thank you for allowing my family and me to stay in the Palace, Your Majesties!" The last part was to King and Queen Huhu who had just come to greet them.

"Why... you're most welcome!" smiled the Queen who was the most beautiful woman that Piperlicious had ever seen.

The presentation would be the next day, but Mom, Dad and Mimi were going to tea with the King and Queen. Mimi asked, "Now, girls, do you want to come and have tea?" Piperlicious said, "No, thank you! We're going to unpack and then explore. We have a plan!"

"Okay," said Mimi. "Be careful then! We'll see you later!"

As soon as the adults had gone, Piperlicious and Londyn watched as their secret friends unloaded themselves. Red Suitcase stretched open, helping Piperlicious to open all the zips, pouches and compartments, then sending all the T-shirts and shorts dancing over the carpet to the drawers Piperlicious would be using, while Brown Bag released everything that had been inside him, with a big sigh of relief!

Unpacking done; the sisters got their super-secret map out. They were going to find the pirate treasure!

Piperlicious had read everything she could about the pirate treasure and told Londyn about it – they would take a boat, find the small treasure island, and bring all the gold and jewels to the King and Queen!

It had originally belonged to the Royal Family, but they had given it all up to fierce Maui warriors for them to use as a ransom to get Princess Luana back from pirates when she was kidnapped, many, many years ago.

"Can I come out now?" asked a muffled voice. It was Paz, who'd been squashed into Piperlicious's pocket all the time!

"Ooh, sorry, Paz!" said Piperlicious guiltily, lifting him out at once, and fluffing him back into shape.

Once out, he shook himself hard, stretched mightily, and then helped with their preparations, pointing out a place to rent a boat, and reminding them to take snacks! Then they set off.

"Aim between Big Island and Maui," said Piperlicious, "towards Mokupuni Akua Island, on the Northern Route."

She was reading the map, while Londyn steered. "We're looking for a Great Hawaiian Warrior, who will let us through if we perform the ritual of the gods."

"What's that?" asked Londyn.
"It's a song," said Piperlicious. "We have to sing a sweet song of some kind."

Paz continued reading about the treasure and the Great Hawaiian Warrior. "He gave the power stones to the people of Maui and guards his secret carefully."

Soon they saw it. The Great Hawaiian Warrior was an immense carving of a Palace Guard, complete with fierce make-up and a big head-dress.

Nervously, Piperlicious began to sing her holiday song. After a moment, Londyn and Paz joined in. It worked! The Warrior sank down beneath the waves, letting them go through!

"Yay!" said Piperlicious.

"Next we have to offer leis to the waters near the three wizards!"

"Wizards?!" exclaimed Londyn.

"Yep!" said Piperlicious, shrugging.

But soon Paz laughed aloud and pointed towards Ola Beach. There, in the doorway of the Rainforest Cave were three stones, each carved to look like a wise man. The three of them: Piperlicious, Londyn, and Paz, each took a lei from the bottom of the boat where they'd placed them and cast it out onto the water. They floated quickly to the beach, each one coming to the foot of a statue, until each wizard had a lei at his feet.

There was a click and a loud grinding sound, and a big round rock rolled aside. Excitedly, they went through the cave which led to a flight of steps, and a very long underground tunnel.

Soon they came to an enormous chest, all tied up with old leather straps. Piperlicious undid the straps, her fingers shaking with excitement, then slowly raised the lid.

Gold, pearls, diamonds, sapphires, rubies, and emeralds gleamed and glittered in the dim light.

"Yay!" cheered Piperlicious and Londyn. "We did it!" They danced around each other, cheering with joy.

Suddenly a light shone down from above. A funny window had opened in the ceiling!

"Who's down there?" asked a voice.

"It can't be... but it sounded like Piperlicious!" It was Mimi's voice!

"It is us!" shouted Piperlicious. "We've found the lost Royal Treasure!"

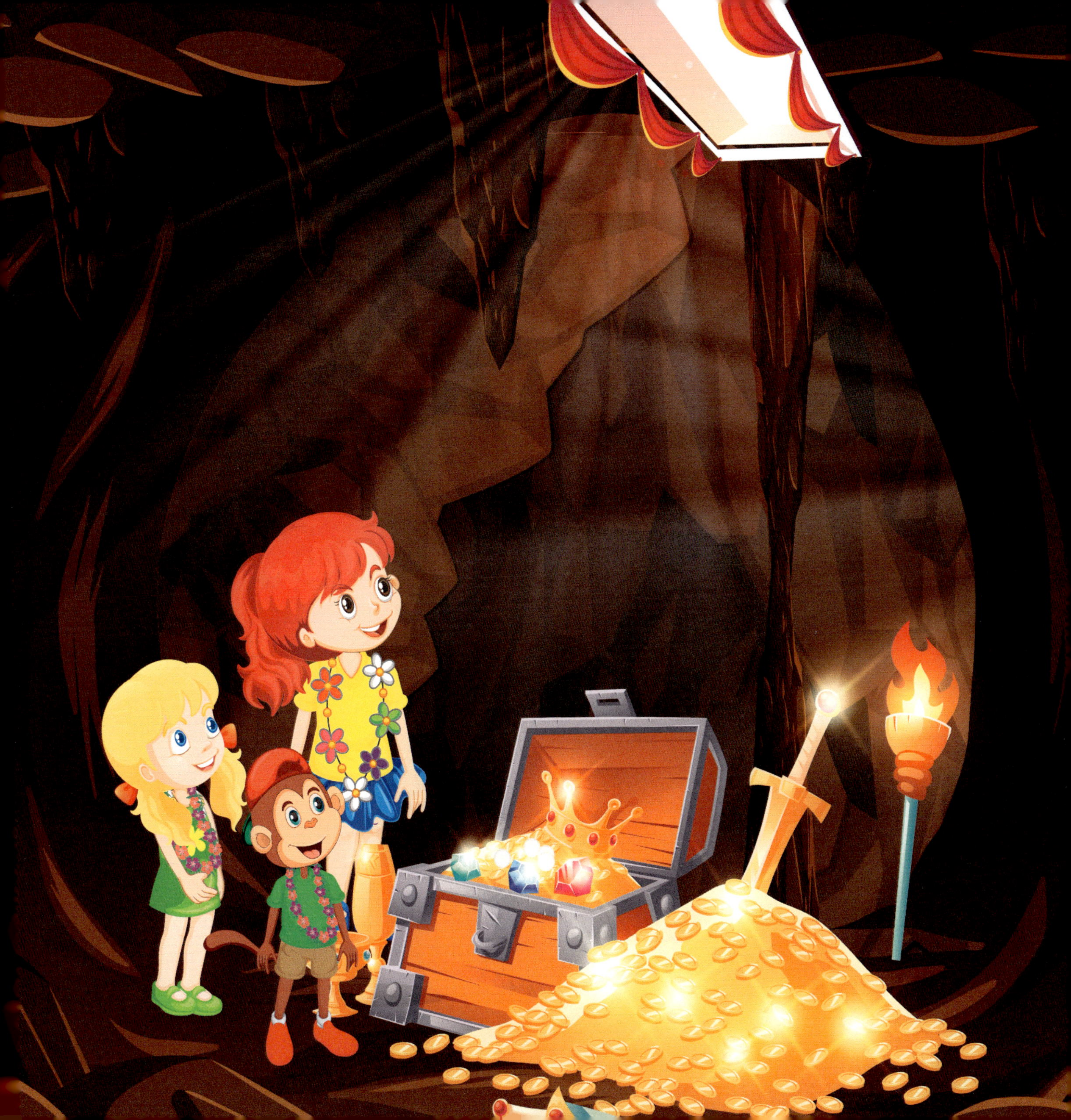

In no time at all, the King had arranged for a ladder and some strong men to carry the treasure up into the Throne Room.

"Goodness me!" he kept saying.

"Imagine the treasure being there this entire time! We thought it was miles away, on the island!"

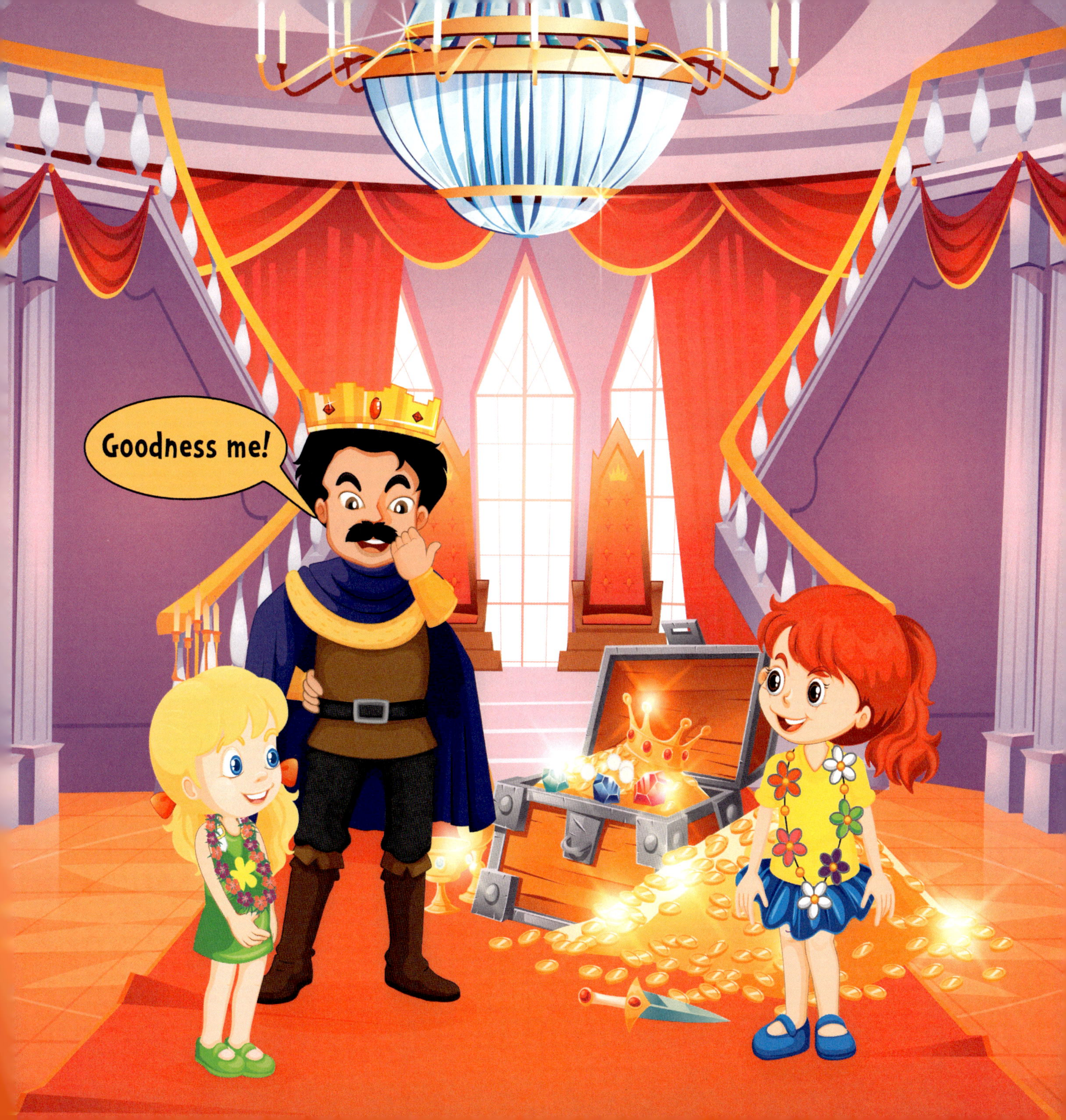
Goodness me!

The Royal Family were so pleased that they called her 'Princess 'O Piperlicious' for the day, and the king gave her a little crown of her very own, that she could keep for always!

She wore her crown for the prize-giving and felt exactly like a princess as she read out the story that she had written.

Princess 'O Piperlicious

Then there was a Princess Ball and luau that everyone in the town was invited to.

Londyn and Piperlicious loved watching Mimi in her grass skirt, dancing all her old hula moves.

When the party was finished, the King and Queen wrote out a big check, there and then, for Piperlicious to give to the charity.

"Thank you," said Piperlicious, over and over again. "Thank you for everything!"

LUAU PARTY

On the plane going home, Mimi asked Piperlicious, "Did you have a good time, then?" Piperlicious snuggled up to her Grandmother, happy but tired, and said, "The very best time ever!"

And every time that Piperlicious went on vacation after that, she made sure she took Paz, and all her secret friends too!

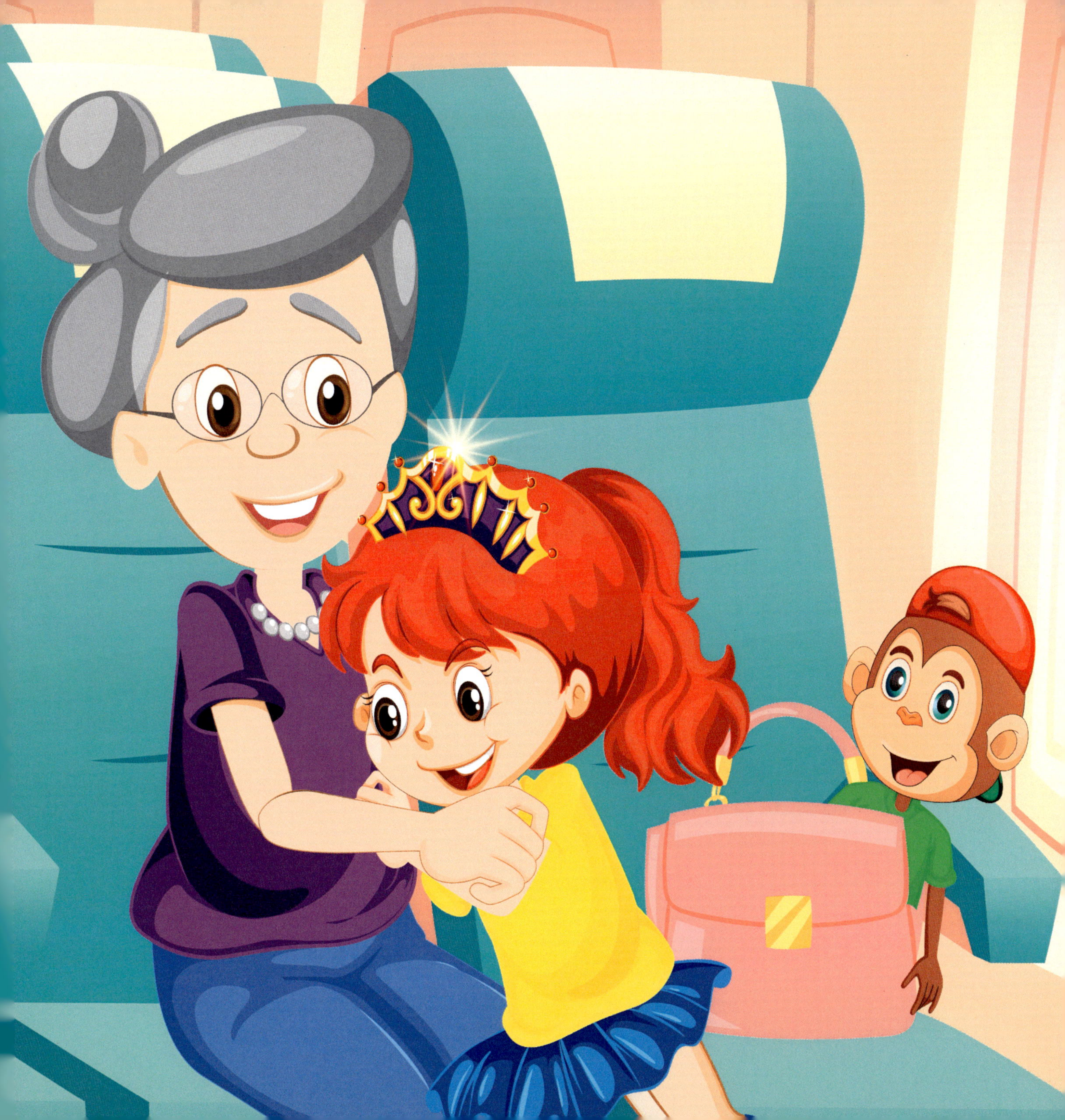

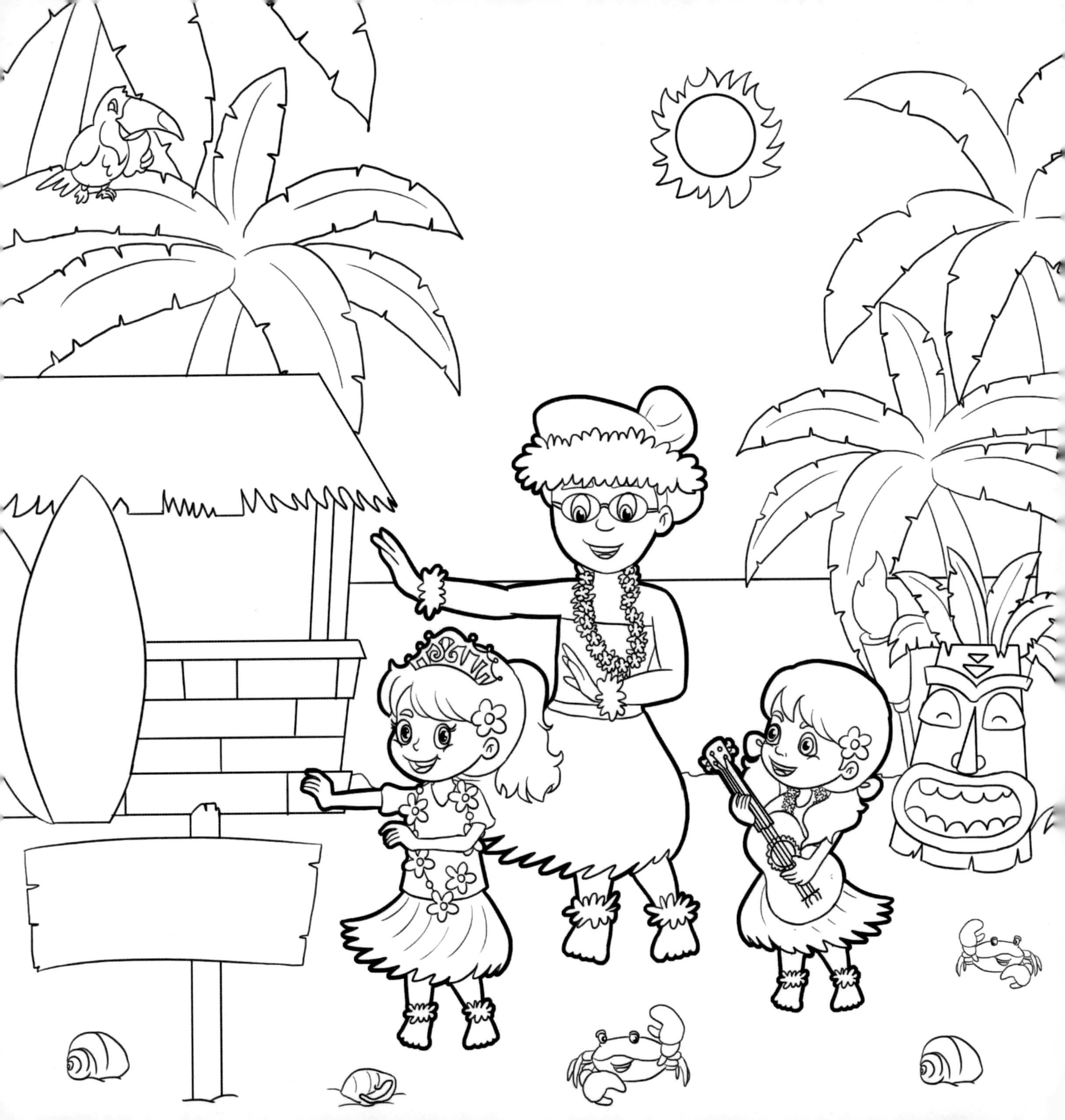

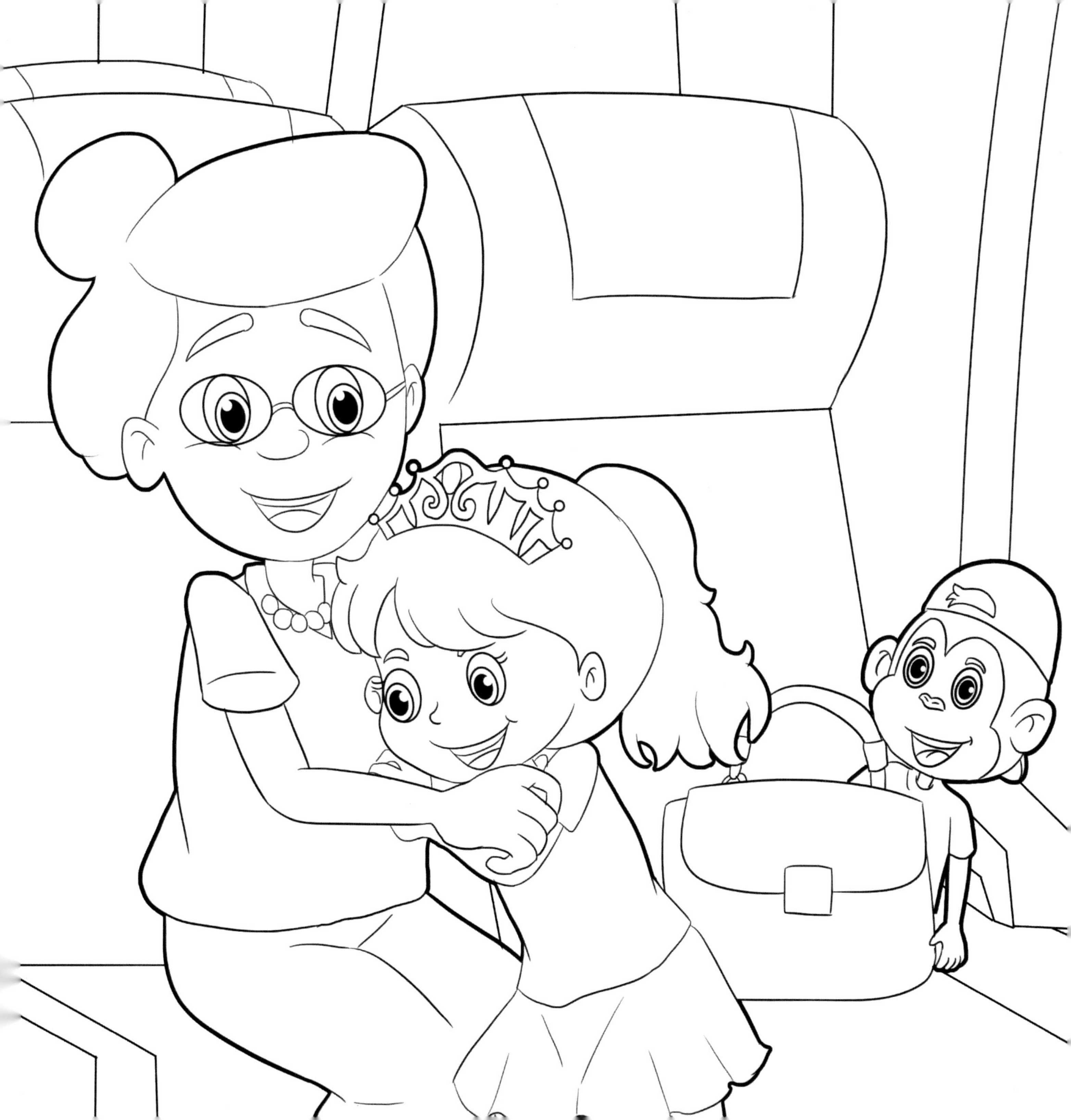

Made in the USA
Monee, IL
09 October 2021